The Laughing Princess

Titles in the series

Kipper and the Giant

Robin Hood

The Laughing Princess

The Shiny Key

Red Planet

Lost in the Jungle

The Laughing Princess

Story by Roderick Hunt

Illustrations by Alex Brychta

OXFORD
UNIVERSITY PRESS

Chip had a new book.

It was about a princess who couldn't laugh.

Nobody could make her laugh.

Chip had an idea.

'Try and make me laugh,' he said.

Biff made a funny face, but she couldn't

make Chip laugh.

Biff put on a funny wig.

She told a funny joke, but she still couldn't

make Chip laugh.

'It's no good,' she said.

Kipper had some joke teeth.

The joke teeth were new.

The teeth went click, click, click.

Everyone laughed and laughed.

The magic key began to glow.

The children ran into Biff's room.

The magic took them on a new adventure.

The children were in a village.

They saw a notice on a tree.

It was about a princess who couldn't laugh.

Kipper had an idea.

He still had the joke teeth.

'I can make the princess laugh,' he said.

The king was in the village.

A girl told him a joke.

'That's not funny,' said the king.

'That won't make the princess laugh.'

'Who's next?' called the king.

'I am,' said a man.

'Oh no!' groaned the king.

'Not another chicken!'

The children went to the king.

'We can make the princess laugh,' said Biff.

'How?' asked the king.

The teeth went click, click, click.

Everyone laughed and laughed.

'That will make the princess laugh,' said the king.

Kipper dropped the teeth.

A dog caught them and ran off with them in its mouth.

'Stop that dog!' shouted the king. 'Stop that dog and get the teeth.'
Everyone ran after the dog.
'Get the teeth!' shouted the king.

The dog was too fast.

Nobody could catch it.

'Stop that dog!' shouted the king.

The dog ran this way and that.

People tried to grab it, but it was too fast.

'Get the teeth!' shouted Kipper.

The king ran after the dog.

Everyone ran after the dog.

The king fell over.

The dog saw a bone and it stopped.

Chip grabbed the dog and the dog dropped
the teeth.

Kipper picked up the joke teeth.

Everyone looked at them.

The teeth were broken.

'Oh no!' said the king.

The king put the teeth on a cushion.

'What a pity!' he said. 'Now they
won't make the princess laugh.'

The princess heard the noise.

She looked out of a window.

She saw the king and she started to laugh.

The king had mud on his clothes.

He had the teeth on the cushion.

He looked so funny that the princess
laughed and laughed.

The king looked at the princess.

'I've made the princess laugh,' he said.

Everyone laughed and cheered.

The magic key began to glow.

The magic took the children home.

But nobody saw the children go.

Everyone was laughing.

'What made the princess laugh?' asked Kipper.

'I don't know,' said Chip, 'but
people laugh at silly things.'

Questions about the story

- Why did Chip ask Biff to make him laugh?
- How did she try to make Chip laugh?
- What did make Biff and Chip laugh?
- Where and when did this Magic Key adventure happen?
- What did the king want someone to do?
- Who were the people who failed?
- Why did Kipper nearly fail?
- What did make the princess laugh in the end?
- Did the children understand what made her laugh?

UNIVERSITY PRESS

Great Clarendon Street, Oxford OX2 6DP

Oxford University Press is a department of the University of Oxford.
It furthers the University's objective of excellence in research, scholarship,
and education by publishing worldwide in

Oxford New York

Athens Auckland Bangkok Bogotá Buenos Aires Calcutta Cape Town
Chennai Dar es Salaam Delhi Florence Hong Kong Istanbul Karachi
Kuala Lumpur Madrid Melbourne Mexico City Mumbai Nairobi
Paris São Paulo Shanghai Singapore Taipei Tokyo Toronto Warsaw

with associated companies in Berlin Ibadan

Oxford is a registered trade mark of Oxford University Press
in the UK and in certain other countries

British Library Cataloguing in Publication Data

Data available

ISBN 0 19 919424 6

Printed in Hong Kong